Glenda Feathers
Casts a Spell

EILEEN CHRISTELOW

Clarion Books

New York

JE   c.1

RD
JUN   1996

The full-color art was created with gouache,
colored pencil, crayon and watercolor.
The text type is 14 pt. ITC Bookman Light.

Clarion Books
a Houghton Mifflin Company imprint
215 Park Avenue South, New York, NY 10003

Text and Illustrations copyright © 1990 by Eileen Christelow

Library of Congress Cataloging-in-Publication Data
Christelow, Eileen.
Glenda Feathers casts a spell/Eileen Christelow.
p.   cm.
Summary: On her first night on the job at Miss Marvel's Witch
Agency, Glenda's inability to keep her spells straight involves her
in a bank robbery and a mad chase to catch the crooks.
ISBN 0-395-51122-4
[1. Witches—Fiction.   2. Magic—Fiction.   3. Robbers and outlaws—
fiction.]   I. Title.
PZ7.C4523G1   1990
[E]—dc20   89-17399
                                                        CIP
                                                         AC

WOZ 10 9 8 7 6 5 4 3 2 1

When Glenda Feathers drove by Miss Marvel's Witch Agency, she noticed a sign in the window. It said HELP WANTED—ADVENTURE AND EXCITEMENT GUARANTEED.

"Oooooh!" said Glenda Feathers. "That's for me!" She parked her car...

...and hurried into the agency.

"I'm here about the job," she told Miss Marvel.

"Can you make it snow in the summer?" asked Miss Marvel. "Make the wind blow on a still day? Open a locked door without a key?"

"Not exactly..." said Glenda Feathers. "But I do learn quickly."

"M-m-m," said Miss Marvel. "I'm desperate for help, so I suppose I should give you a chance. But I have my doubts."

She gave Glenda Feathers a uniform, a broom, and a handbook of spells.

"This is so exciting," said Glenda Feathers. "Adventures! Late nights riding on a broom in a moonlit sky!"

"Not so fast," said Miss Marvel. "First, let's see if you can even cast a good spell!"

She showed Glenda Feathers how to cast a spell
that would open a locked door without a key.

She showed her how to make it snow, and how to
make the wind blow.

"It looks so easy!" said Glenda Feathers.

"For some it is. For most it isn't," said Miss Marvel.

Glenda Feathers tried to cast the spell that opens locked doors.

BANG! The door popped off its hinges.

Then a strong wind blasted through the room, and snow swirled around them.

"No! No! No!" shouted Miss Marvel. "You're mixing up the spells!"

"Ooops!" said Glenda Feathers.

By the end of the day, Glenda Feathers was still mixing up spells.

"Face it," said Miss Marvel. "This job is not for you."

"Give me just one more chance!" pleaded Glenda Feathers.

"Well, there is a job you could probably do," said Miss Marvel. She left Glenda Feathers to answer the phone while she and the other witches went out to cast spells.

"So much for excitement and adventure," groaned Glenda Feathers. But just then, two customers walked in. They said their names were Bernie and Phyllis.

"Can you do two door unlocking spells right away?" asked Phyllis. "We lost our keys."

"I think I can," said Glenda Feathers. "But..."

"So, what are we waiting for?" said Bernie.

Glenda Feathers left a note for Miss Marvel. Then she rode away with Bernie and Phyllis. While they were driving, she studied the door unlocking spell in her handbook.

"This could be my big chance," she thought to herself.

They parked behind a large brick building.

"Isn't this the bank?" asked Glenda Feathers.

"Yup," said Bernie. "We work here at night."

"And we're late," said Phyllis. "Because we lost our keys."

"I hope I can help you get in," said Glenda Feathers.

She closed her eyes and cast the door unlocking spell. Then she held her breath.

The door swung open.

"Miss Marvel should see this!" said Glenda
Feathers.

Phyllis rushed into the bank. "There's another
door inside. Hurry! It's starting to snow."

"How can it be snowing?" asked Bernie. "It's
summer."

"Ooops!" Glenda Feathers said to herself.

They followed Phyllis inside to a huge metal door.
"Isn't this where they keep the money?" asked
Glenda Feathers.
"Yup," said Bernie. "Our job is to count it."

"I don't know if the spell works on this kind of
door," said Glenda Feathers.
She closed her eyes and cast the spell.

The heavy metal door creaked open.

"Would you look at all that cash?" whispered Phyllis.

"Hey!" shouted Bernie. "Where's that wind coming from?"

"Ooops!" groaned Glenda Feathers.

"It's blowing all the cash around," shouted Bernie.

"Shhhhhh!" hissed Phyllis. She snatched a sack out of her purse. "Don't make so much noise, or we'll be caught for sure."

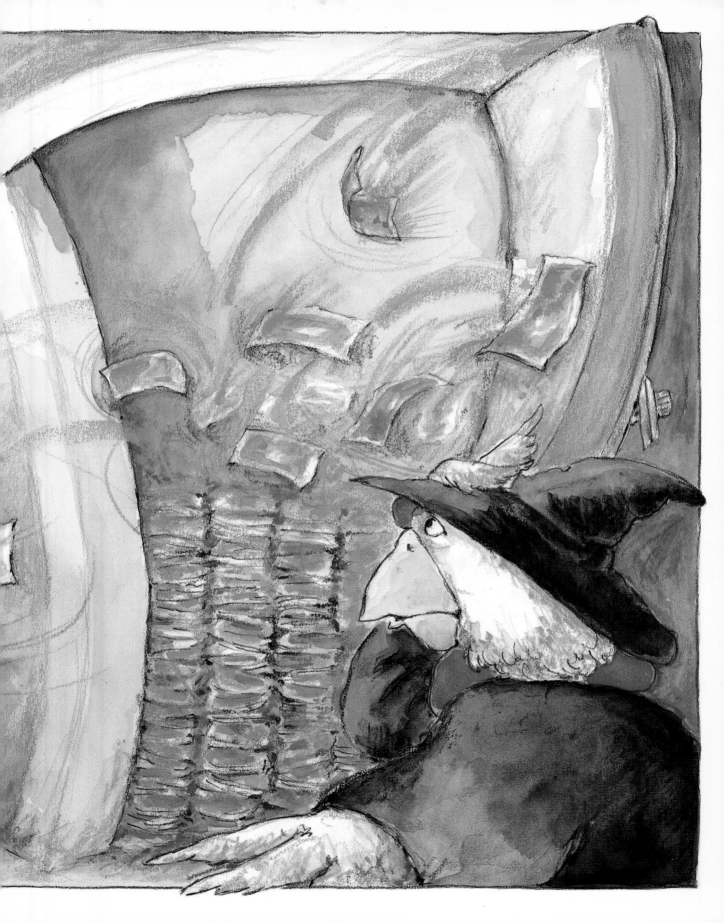

"Caught?" whispered Glenda Feathers. "Oh no! Bernie and Phyllis must be bank robbers!"

Bernie and Phyllis were trying to stuff the sack with money.

"It's blowing away!" shouted Bernie.

"Catch it!" shrieked Phyllis.

"This is my chance," thought Glenda Feathers.
She crept over to the burglar alarm and pulled the lever.

"The alarm!" cried Phyllis. "Let's beat it!"
She grabbed the sack of money. Bernie grabbed
Glenda Feathers, and they tore out of the bank.

"Am I dreaming?" gasped Bernie. "Our car is
buried in snow! We're trapped!"
"Never!" said Phyllis. "I'll drive. The bird can
push."

"Good idea!" said Bernie. He and Phyllis jumped
into the car. Phyllis started the engine.

"If only I could lock them in," Glenda Feathers
muttered. "Well, it can't hurt to try."

She closed her eyes and cast the door *unlocking*
spell *backward*.

When she opened her eyes, Bernie and Phyllis
were gone. All that was left was the sack of money.

"They got away!" she gasped. She tried to open the
car door. It was locked.

Then she heard Bernie's voice…inside the car.

"Don't just stand there! Let us out!"

"Ooops!" groaned Glenda Feathers. "They're invisible!"

Then someone behind her shouted, "Put up your wings! It's the police!"

"Thank goodness!" said Glenda Feathers.

But the policeman locked a handcuff on her wing.

"You're making a mistake!" cried Glenda Feathers. "I didn't rob the bank. I work for Miss Marvel's Witch Agency and I just trapped the robbers in that car!"

"Lady, no one is in the car," said the policeman.

"You don't understand," said Glenda Feathers. "They're invisible!"

"Tell that to the chief," said the policeman.

He took Glenda Feathers to the police station and the car was towed to the police parking lot to be held as evidence.

Glenda Feathers told her story to the chief.
"This is very confusing," he said.

Just then Miss Marvel hurried into the room.

"I'm glad you policemen called," she said. "I'm sorry I ever hired this bird. I left her to answer the phone, and what did she do? She took off and robbed a bank!"

"Wait a minute!" shouted Glenda Feathers. "I didn't rob the bank! I cast a spell and *captured* the robbers. But no one believes me because somehow I made them invisible..."

"That figures," said Miss Marvel.

"Look out the window!" interrupted the policeman. "That car is driving itself away!"

"After it!" shouted the chief.

Everyone jumped into a police car. With lights flashing and sirens screaming, they chased after the fleeing car. The car swerved to the left...

...and crashed into a fence.

The policeman jumped out of his car.

"You're under arrest!" he shouted.

"Who is?" asked the chief.

"Just a minute," said Glenda Feathers. "I think I can help." She looked quickly in the handbook of spells.

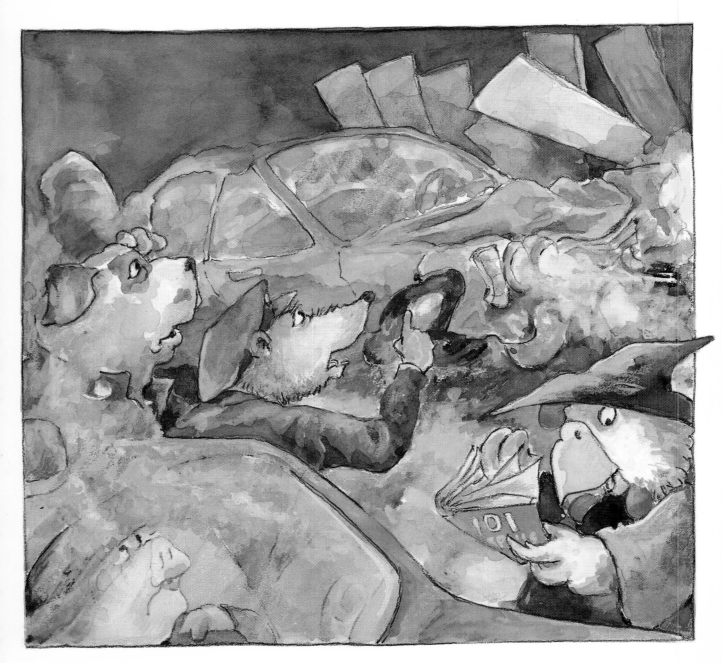

"Don't!" shouted Miss Marvel. "Wait!"

But Glenda Feathers closed her eyes and cast one more spell.

There was a puff of pink smoke.

"Now you've done it!" said Miss Marvel.

But when the smoke cleared, everyone gasped. "Bernie and Phyllis!" said the policeman. "We've been looking for these crooks for months! But… what happened to the car?"

"Don't stand there asking stupid questions," said the chief. "Handcuff those two. And hurry, it's starting to snow!"

"Ooops!" said Glenda Feathers.